Louise enjoys watching her words come to life in her books like many other people. While she's not flying in helicopters, she spends her time coming up with stories to share with the world.

Getting Ready for

Christmas

L. A. Meagher

AUSTIN MACAULEY PUBLISHERS™

LONDON * CAMBRIDGE * NEW YORK * SHARJAH

Ordering Information:
Quantity sales: special discounts are available on quantity purchases by corporations, associations, and others. For details, contact the publisher at the address below.

Meagher, L. A.
Getting Ready for Christmas

ISBN 9781641825573 (Paperback)
ISBN 9781641825580 (Hardback)
ISBN 9781641825597 (E-Book)

The main category of the book — JUVENILE FICTION / Holidays & Celebrations / Christmas & Advent

www.austinmacauley.com/us

First Published (2018)
Austin Macauley Publishers LLC
40 Wall Street, 28th Floor
New York, NY 10005
USA

mail-usa@austinmacauley.com
+1 (646) 5125767

I dedicate this book to ALL of my family, for all the wonderful Christmas memories we have shared together.

Are you getting excited? It's finally here! **Christmas** time is coming.

It's the best time of the year!

On **December 1st**, take a look all around. You will see the bustle and hear the sounds.

Christmas is coming and coming fast. It's a favorite time, let's hope it will last!

6

December 2nd, a cold wind blows. It makes the eyes water and chills the nose. It's time for gloves, a coat, and a hat. Your boots and scarf... Yes, time for that.

8

December 3rd comes and have you heard? **Christmas** music is playing.

Let's sing every word.

Some people go shopping from store to store. As we hang a wreath on the front door.

It's **December 4th**, and in our children's eyes I can see, today is the day
to put up the tree.

A little early for some but never for them. We give the children a nod and
they give back a grin.

It's the **5th of December**; the tree has been trimmed. You plug in the lights as the main lights are dimmed.

The tree twinkles and shines with a heavenly angel on top. It's one of those moments you wish would not stop.

14

December 6th is a day that children sit down. To write their dear Santa
so he'll stop in their town.
They ask him for toys or a kitten with soft paws, then they tell him they love
their dear Santa Clause.

December **7th** is a day to watch **Christmas** shows, like Rudolph the reindeer
with his shiny red nose!
There's *Frosty, The Grinch* or even *A Christmas Story*.
This time of year is never boring.

18

The plan for today on **December 8th** is to make **Christmas** cookies to put out on plates.
We cut them in shapes after we roll out the dough. Dad always steals one. It's tradition, you know!

Poinsettias white or red, a **Christmas** cactus that is pink. Wonderful colors all around. It's amazing, don't you think?

The excitement and joy of **December 9th** are in the air. People are helping people and showing that they care.

22

What will we do on the 10th of December? So many things, it's hard to remember.
Let's get our cards ready and seal them with a kiss. To send everyone love and wish
them a Merry Christmas!

24

It's **December 11th**, and as you look out the window, there on the ground is some fluffy white snow.
Just a few inches more, try to wait if you can. Then go right out there and build a snowman.

26

December 12th brings **Christmas** dances, pageants, and plays. There's so much to do.
We don't have enough days.
The kids will dress up in their costumes or frills. It's exciting to watch all
the boys and the girls.

28

It's **December 13th** and today is halfway to celebrating another
magical **Christmas** day!
It's still as exciting to me, as back on day one. With only 11 days left to get
our shopping all done.

Counting down the days OF
DECEMBER
2018

SUNDAY	MONDAY	TUESDAY	WEDNESDAY	THURSDAY	FRIDAY	SATURDAY
~~1~~	~~2~~	~~3~~	~~4~~	~~5~~	~~6~~	~~7~~
~~8~~	~~9~~	~~10~~	~~11~~	~~12~~	~~13~~	14
15	16	17	18	19	20	21
22	23	24	25	26	27	28
29	30	31				

Let's go for a drive to look at the lights. Then we'll stop at the park for

a brief snowball fight.

December 14th is for making memories; ones we'll cherish for years.

Having so much fun as we laugh till there are tears.

Come **December 15th**, we will go out to see, dear old Santa himself and
climb on his knee.
A whisper in his ear to ask for things on our list. Then we check once with Mom to
make sure there's nothing we missed.

Let's find us a hill for our toboggans and sleds. **December 16th** is not a day to stay in our beds. Our cheeks will get rosy our faces will glow, and when we get home, I bet there'll be cocoa.

A **Christmas** party we should have on **December 17th**. Invite the young and the old and everyone in between.

We'll have eggnog and sing carols by a fireside glow as some will steal a kiss under the mistletoe.

On **December 18th**, stand outside and listen, amid the ice and the snow while the moonlight glistens.

In the distance, you might hear some church or sleigh bells, as the sounds of **Christmas** make your heart swell.

You'll feel like a kid while you build a gingerbread house. When you sneak a gumdrop piece, be sure you're quiet as a mouse.

Use all the colors of **Christmas**; silver, gold, red, and green. There are only six days left as today is **December 19th**.

42

It's time now to see Grandma, and you know how that song goes. She gets you the things you want for Christmas. How is it that she knows? It's December 20th, just five days more. Till wrapping paper and toys will cover the floor.

The elves are all watching the girls and the boys. While Santa's workshop is busy building all of the toys.

It's December 21st. It's almost here. Make sure you have carrots to leave for the reindeer!

Candy canes have been hanging from garland and trees. You may have one, yes, if you ask with a please?

The excitement is building on **December 22**. Have you hung up your stockings for you know who?

On **December 23rd**, the tinsel will sparkle as the candles burn bright.

The stars are all twinkling in the still of the night.

The snowflakes fall slowly, only two days to go, as anticipation is building

and it grows and grows.

It's finally **Christmas** Eve, **December 24th**. The night the man dressed in red comes from way up north.

When Santa comes to see you, make sure that you're asleep. He knows if you are peeking so your promise you must keep.

Close your eyes and dream of him, and in the morning when you wake, you'll find the things you asked for on that list that you did make.

December 25th! **Christmas** Day is here, and it's as amazing as we thought.
Remember though, that **Christmas** isn't about the things we got.
Christmas is about believing more than what your eyes may see. It's more than just the gifts that Santa leaves beneath the tree.
Getting ready for **Christmas** and preparing for this day, should include some love and laughter and be enjoyed along the way.
Merry **Christmas** to you all and a Happy New Year too! Enjoy your many blessings every day the whole year through!